The Shopping Expedition

André Amstutz

The Shopping Expedition

words by Allan Ahlberg

First U.S. edition 2005

Library of Congress Cataloging-in-Publication Data

Ahlberg, Allan.
The shopping expedition / by Allan Ahlberg ; illustrated by André Amstutz. —1st U.S. ed.
p. cm.
Summary: A routine shopping trip becomes a grand adventure in the eyes of a little girl.
ISBN 0-7636-2586-8
[1. Imagination—Fiction. 2. Shopping—Fiction.] I. Amstutz, André, ill. II. Title.
PZ7.A2688Sh 2005
[E]—dc22   2003069674

10 9 8 7 6 5 4 3 2 1

Printed in China

This book was typeset in FC Kennerly Regular.
The illustrations were done in acrylic.

Candlewick Press
2067 Massachusetts Avenue
Cambridge, Massachusetts 02140

visit us at www.candlewick.com

CANDLEWICK PRESS
CAMBRIDGE, MASSACHUSETTS

That was the day
that Mom and I
and little Harry
and Wilf the Wonderdog
went shopping.
Mom made her usual list:

Cornflakes
Milk
Sausages
apples – eggs
Toothpaste
Dog biscuits
Orange juice
baby powder
Bread

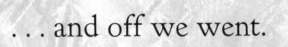

. . . and off we went.

On the way, the car broke down,
but we kept going.

The rain came down,
but we kept going.

The road got steeper . . .

and steeper.

The *snow* came down, the wind blew up a blizzard,

and Wilf the Wonderdog pulled us along.

The sun came out.

The road got narrower . . .

and twistier . . .

and greener.

But we kept going.

The *jungle* got thicker,

but we kept going.

Mom saved us
from the snakes.
Wilf saved us
from the crocodiles.
I saved us from the
cheeky monkeys.

The road became a river,

but we kept going.

The river became . . .

a sea!

The sea rose and fell and washed
us to the shore.

Yes,
that was the day—
and the night—
that Mom and I
and little Harry
and Wilf the Wonderdog
went shopping . . .

to the shop on
the shore.

And it was still . . .

OPEN

The End